HUNTED

OUTRUN. OUTLAST. OUTWIT.

Tales From The UK

Edited By Megan Roberts

First published in Great Britain in 2020 by:

Young Writers
Remus House
Coltsfoot Drive
Peterborough
PE2 9BF
Telephone: 01733 890066
Website: www.youngwriters.co.uk

Printed and bound in the UK by BookPrintingUK
Website: www.bookprintinguk.com
YB0439A

FOREWORD

IF YOU'VE BEEN SEARCHING FOR EPIC ADVENTURES, TALES OF SUSPENSE AND IMAGINATIVE WRITING THEN SEARCH NO MORE! YOUR HUNT IS AT AN END WITH THIS ANTHOLOGY OF MINI SAGAS.

We challenged secondary school students to craft a story in just 100 words. In this first installment of our SOS Sagas, their mission was to write on the theme of 'Hunted'. But they weren't restricted to just predator vs prey, oh no. They were encouraged to think beyond their first instincts and explore deeper into the theme.

The result is a variety of styles and genres and, as well as some classic cat and mouse games, inside these pages you'll find characters looking for meaning, people running from their darkest fears or maybe even death itself on the hunt.

Here at Young Writers it's our aim to inspire the next generation and instill in them a love for creative writing, and what better way than to see their work in print? The imagination and skill within these pages are proof that we might just be achieving that aim! Well done to each of these fantastic authors.

So if you're ready to find out if the hunter will become the hunted, read on!

CONTENTS

Lucy Smith (14)	64
Kalib Blair (14)	65
Reece Hooper (14)	66
Erin Joan MacGregor (14)	67
Abby Clarke (14)	68
Grace Galloway (13)	69
Nathan Rodgers (13)	70
Hollie Macnamara (13)	71
Jane Macmillan (14)	72
Sean Allen (13)	73
Jamie Roddie (13)	74
Ayley Crawford (14)	75
Abigail Craig (13)	76

Dean Trust Rose Bridge, Ince-In-Makerfield

Skye Elizabeth Myers Burney (11)	77
Simon Doodson-Smith (14)	78
Amelia Southall (11)	79
Kaitlyn Cox (11)	80

Homewood College, Brighton

| Sam Simmons (15) | 81 |

Onslow St Audrey's School, Hatfield

| Lacey Harwood (12) | 82 |

Ryde Academy, Ryde

Riley Shaw (11)	83
Callum Winter (12)	84
Scarlett de Havilland (13)	85
Evie Thomas (12)	86
Ella Crowther (13)	87
Emma Noble (13)	88
Alesha Roberts (13)	89
Becca Aspden (13)	90
Ben Moralee (12)	91
Bam Ruth	92
Danny Wilson (14)	93

Rhys Mundell (14)	94
Taya Cotton (11)	95
Caitlin Jessica John (12)	96
Sara Setzu (12)	97
Kayleigh Batchelor (14)	98
Erica Roberts (13)	99
George Hiorns (12)	100
Nathan Day (13)	101
Lillie Ghetty-Evans (13)	102
Chloe Cowans (13)	103
Ewan Gascoigne (12)	104
Amelia Day (11)	105
Violet Slimm (11)	106
Brooke De'ath (12)	107
Tilly Nicholls (13)	108
Nathan Arnold-Recalde (13)	109
Lloyd Nicholls (11)	110
Kacie Hodgson (12)	111
Leo Stone (11)	112
Joseph Paice-Jones (12)	113
Grace Nicholls	114
Violet Paxton	115
Khaila Hill-Crewe (11)	116
Emily Ainsworth (11)	117
Beau Bowden (11)	118
Kelly Morgan (12)	119
Monika Bielik (11)	120
Matthew Artress-Brown (13)	121
Christopher Sillito (13)	122
Amalie Yardley (11)	123
Megan Pugmire (14)	124
Jacob Coates (12)	125
Robyn Moody (12)	126
Madison Bloomfield (12)	127
Hayley Louise Molloy (11)	128
Nikita Henry-Gorshanov (12)	129
Lewis Woolven (13)	130
Hazel Dawn Everard (13)	131
Isaac Turvey (12)	132
Isabelle Bull (13)	133
Preston George Groves	134
Jasper Irvine	135
Crystal-Rose Griffiths (13)	136

Maciej Sadel (11)	137
Carla Harrison (13)	138
Ellie Carbin (14)	139
Jake Mander (13)	140
Jacob Orme (11)	141
Jack Schubert (11)	142
Jay Rayson	143
Sammy Gallimore (11)	144
Pixie-Rose Sunshine Gardner (12)	145
Toby Seddon	146
Aidan Partridge (13)	147
Chloe Powell (13)	148
Jacob Patterson (14)	149
Tyria Lake (14)	150
Katie Taylor (14)	151

St Catherine's College, Eastbourne

Gurleen Kaur (13)	152
Lois Katie Hilton (15)	153

Victoria Education Centre, Branksome Park

Josh Bolton (18)	154
Elisha Robinson (17)	155
Christopher Jones (17)	156
Louis Meddelton (16)	157
Charlotte Sharpe (17)	158
Deniz Akgul (13)	159

Woking High School, Horsell

Imaniya Hussain (11)	160
Sana Newa Khan (11)	161
Chloe Isabella Barwick (11)	162

THE STORIES

The Evil Always Follows

Sharp wails cut through the air as the woman frantically rushed forward, a baby in her arms. A snap was heard and the baby fell to the floor, motionless. She carried on regardless, though the tears were now streaming down her cheeks. Somebody cut in front of her and she screamed in desperation. How could she leave him? He was everywhere, following her. She had to get out, but the gun in her hand rose upwards. A loud boom resounded and she fell to the floor, dead. Her body lay there for ten days before somebody finally noticed...

Jessica Austin (16)
Alleyne's Academy, Stone

Red-Eyed Wolf

Red-eyed wolves sped up after me. Choking for breath, I ran for my life. My house was fifty metres away. I didn't think I could make it. I grabbed a branch and threw it at one. We were close... I couldn't run for much longer. It was the end... I couldn't give in yet. Something got into me and my strength came back. I ran into the house and locked the door. I survived. They nearly broke my door but I'd survived. My dogs that lived outside didn't make it...

Elmira Bahareva (15)
Alleyne's Academy, Stone

Escaped Convict

We only had twenty minutes before the sirens wailed. We were on the run. My hips were stinging. My lips were burning. I listened and heard the sirens wailing. My mind was blank. We were heading straight for a dead end. I was about to give up when a police car pulled up right behind me. Then, something dashed past me. I couldn't give up just yet. I ran for my life, but then I heard a *psst!* I quickly went over to this mysterious man...

Faith Hallie Sweetman (15)
Alleyne's Academy, Stone

Time Is Ticking

Time was against me. One minute left and I'd barely started. I failed to stay in the time limit every time. It hunted me down every time. It tore me apart every time. Just this once, I absolutely had to beat it. Halfway through and thirty seconds left. "Just keep going," that was what I kept telling myself. "Just keep going, nearly there now... Last little bit..." *Ten! Nine!* I was running out of time. *Eight! Seven! Six!* I was preparing to dismount. *Five! Four!* I dismounted with a second to spare. It was all over. Relief ran through me...

Mia Charlton (11)
Colne Valley High School, Linthwaite

Alien Run

Multicoloured lights flashed around me, creating miniature circles on the ground. A beam of white light glowed, covering me. Slipping on the ice-covered pavements, I ran through all the shadowy deserted streets, but the glistening silver machine was still following me like it was trying to hunt me down. All of a sudden, I heard what sounded like squelchy footsteps. I turned around. Behind me were lime-green human frog-like creatures. I looked up and then I saw them jumping out of the metal machine that was following me. I kept running, but those unidentified things were following me...

Holly Davenport (11)
Colne Valley High School, Linthwaite

It Never Stops

Dashing towards the clearing, I halted. Where was it? It was a ferocious, horrendous, hideous creature. Its vile teeth ripped through my mind. Rigid, black, wiry fur was a veil over the past. Then, I heard it, the scamper of its claws. Frantically, I headed away from the clearing, deciding it was a trap. Suddenly, I scrambled up the nearest, tallest tree. Cautiously, I relaxed, a booming growl came from its jaws of death, rattling my cowering core. Dead eyes peered through me as it climbed higher and higher and higher. Petrified to stone, blood dripped upon my quaking head...

Kayleigh Lawton (14)
Colne Valley High School, Linthwaite

Was... That...?

In the middle of a forest, no escape, and two deep, dark eyes stared right into your soul. Many trees enclosed you and your thoughts went into a dark place. Silence filled the air, a familiar voice echoing in your mind. A derelict cabin stood in the distance, an eerie darkness swallowing it with one gulp. Walking to running, it was following you, turning your insides out. It seemed like... it couldn't be... skinwalkers. Turning that small run into a sprint, you weren't going to get away. Slowly, the cabin came closer, but it was too late. You'd been hunted...

Caitlin Summer Walland (11)
Colne Valley High School, Linthwaite

The Alaska Hunt

It's hunting season in Alaska and ten men have to hunt the rare purple feathered turkey. Whoever winds gets £100,000 Christmas shopping money. They've been split up into teams, the red team and the blue team. Each team has to split the money. If they win, every person on the team will win £20,000 each. The teams will start hunting at 8:15 tonight at Jolly Jolly Street. They will be making their way around the country, shooting turkeys and asking people if they've seen this famous turkey. They can eat it, but they cannot disobey the law...

Lennon Avison (12)
Colne Valley High School, Linthwaite

The Doll

I was running, running as fast as ever, running from her. All these years thinking that I was the one hunting her when I was actually the one being hunted. Darting through the looming trees, I heard cackles of mad laughter, the mistress of doom herself forever on my tail. Above, the glaring moon hid dangerously behind the grey streaks through the sky, barely worthy of being called clouds. The wind slapped my frozen cheek or was it her, beating her cracked porcelain against my skin? I stopped and looked. She had hunted and she had definitely, painfully succeeded.

Gracie Bucknell (11)
Colne Valley High School, Linthwaite

When They Came

Everything was perfect, everything was great before they came. Local snatchers were out seeking children to be swallowed by their cruel hands. Little did we know, they were part of something much bigger than we thought. They caught fifty children that night: I was one of them.

Once I'd regained my consciousness, my mind was empty except for the word: run. I did. I ran through a maze of corrugated iron and crumbling stone. My legs and mind were racing faster than ever before, too fast to comprehend where I was or remember that I couldn't escape the maze...

George Bolton (11)
Colne Valley High School, Linthwaite

The Bottomless Pit

What were they thinking? This would take their lives in an instant if they weren't careful. Eerie darkness filled the wood's perimeter. Step by step, the girls pounded across the sludgy earth, pinching their noses tight. All of a sudden, they came to a halt. A shadowy pit drew their attention. One step and they were gone, forever never to be seen, their precious smiles would be kept in a pit of never-ending nothingness. It was so quiet, you could hear echoing coming from far down. *Bang!* Where had they gone? No one knew from this day...

Ruby Hartwell (11)
Colne Valley High School, Linthwaite

The Day I Nearly Died...

The moon shone over me, creating an eerie shadow. There was a cacophony of sound in the melancholic atmosphere. I could hear twigs snapping behind me. I immediately knew he was here. As it munched slowly on the leaves, I couldn't blink in case I missed something. I stood over the valley as if it was untouchable, waiting. I was stood over the valley, expecting something to happen. I was wrong. I only just made it in time. I saw something I wished I'd never experienced. It didn't just appear, it stayed there. That was the day I nearly died...

Layla-Mae Kidger (11)
Colne Valley High School, Linthwaite

Hide-And-Seek

As I was walking towards the abandoned church, we decided to go and play hide-and-seek. Suddenly, I heard a noise. It was like a bang, like someone was looking at me through the window. Ten minutes later, I was hiding under a table with creepy spiders and cobwebs. I couldn't hear any of my friends. I thought to myself, *where could they have gone?* Suddenly, I heard whispering... Could it be my friends? No, it wasn't. It was a man with no face. It was stuck like a mouldy old statue. I then went to find my lost friends...

Ada Burnett (11)
Colne Valley High School, Linthwaite

Hunted

My feet were as silent as a still night in the barren fields of Yorkshire. The sirens were blinding and they deafened me. It was overwhelming. Drops of innocent, salty tears ran down my burning cheek as I ran into the dark woodland which inhabited all sorts of rabid rodents which could strike at any second. There were a million intricate knots tangled in my stomach and my heart beat out of my chest. Ice-cold my hands were. My legs began to get heavier. Stopping to hide, I saw it under a pile of leaves. I hid, invisible...

Isabelle Thornton (11)
Colne Valley High School, Linthwaite

Dark Assassin

I hid behind a tree, listening for the assassin's footsteps. My heart felt like it was outside my body. Suddenly, I heard a branch snap above me. Frantically, my legs stood up. Looking around, I saw a dark, gloomy figure run through the trees. It was here and there was nowhere to run except into a sharp-bladed knife. When I turned around, my eyes met with the killer, her dark black hair dangled in front of the bloodshot eyes. There was nothing I could do but I still tried to run. The knife then reached its target...

Aaron Henry Carlton (11)
Colne Valley High School, Linthwaite

On The Run

As I sprinted down the road, the rumble of helicopters pounding my ears flew. Up ahead was the slow clank of tanks, at least it sounded like it. I realised what planet I'd crashed onto... Earth. I asked my droid BD-1 to do a perimeter scan. *Beep boop!* I pulled out my lightsaber. I could sense footsteps up ahead. They'd followed me, the entire Sith army. Suddenly, I was surrounded by red lightsabers. Darth Vader, Kylo Ren, the Emperor, Darth Sideous, Count Dooku... I was trapped. I'd have to fight...

Oscar John Searle (14)
Colne Valley High School, Linthwaite

Friendship Of The Beasts

The dragon snarled. The sound of pain covered the valley in noise as the sharp, jagged spear pierced through the monster's scaled chest. Its shiny blue eyes shrank as the feeling of death devoured its body, making it collapse to the ground. In a rush of fear, the dragon squealed for help, but then in a flash, the almighty yellow griffin dived from the sky, roaring in anger. The puny humans ran for their lives as the yellow griffin came out, glorious and victorious. That didn't stop the suffering of the dragon...

Connah James Phillips (11)
Colne Valley High School, Linthwaite

Escape

The police were hot on my tail. Trees stood on the ground, being my only chance at survival. Early in the morning, the police banged on doors, searching for me as if they were lions that hadn't eaten for days. I scoured the area in the cold, bleak rain, hiding myself from the police. My ears could hear them breathing down my neck. My heart was pounding. Heart beating, I sprinted through the nearby small village. The village was in sight. I could get out of the police's radar. I thought to myself and ran. I was close...

Joshua Kenyon (12)
Colne Valley High School, Linthwaite

The Man In The Bunker

It was a damp night in 1943 in Nazi Germany. I had secret intel and everyone was out to get me. *Bang!* Suddenly, the ground shook like an earthquake. A shell had gone off next to my underground bunker. Over the last few days, the Germans had been on the retreat. All of a sudden, there was a knock at the door. I answered it, careful in case the Germans came through the door. Sure enough, they burst through and captured me. I tried to get out of their tight grip, but I couldn't. Then, they took everything...

Liam Ambler (11)
Colne Valley High School, Linthwaite

Run

Vicious claws scraped against the floor and that was when I knew I had to run. Running as fast as a spreading disease, I dodged the sharp rocks blocking my escape. Panting heavily, I leapt onto the rough floor, calling for help. Dripping from my fur, sweat rolled down my bloody face. My heart filled with fear, I was no longer able to carry the weight of my body. Collapsing under the rock, the sun was a ball of fire making it a lot harder to run for my life. I was officially hunted. There was nothing left to do...

Esme Beatrice Dawson (11)
Colne Valley High School, Linthwaite

I Couldn't Run For Much Longer!

I couldn't run for much longer, I felt like animals were hunting me. The trees looked like they were reaching out to get me. I saw eyes staring into my soul, there was no escape. I was worrying so much, I didn't know what to do. I was with my friend, we didn't know where our parents were. I was so terrified. There was a castle in the woods. I thought to myself, *why is there a castle in the woods?* So we went in and we couldn't escape. We started to lose our things as we tried to escape...

Amelia Dennison (12)
Colne Valley High School, Linthwaite

The Snapping Sticks

I could hear a whistling sound following me. I kept on turning around. I could hear things but I couldn't see anything. I was terrified. I could hear footsteps walking closer, closer and closer to me. I started to shake. I stood there, watching around me. I could hear sticks snapping, heavy breathing getting closer and closer. The trees were moving in the wind. I started to shiver. I was shivering and shivering and I started to shake. I felt like I could fall to the ground. I could hear growling far behind me...

Gracie Clifford (12)
Colne Valley High School, Linthwaite

The Hunt Mission

I couldn't run for much longer, I could feel my heart pounding inside me. Twigs snapped under my feet, then silence fell upon the air. I looked around; everything looked the same. I didn't know where I was. All of a sudden. I heard the loud thudding noise of horse hooves. I couldn't wait much longer, I had to go. I ran as fast as I could. They were catching up to me. Faster, faster I ran. A tree root reached and grabbed my ankle. Then, I fell to the floor. Quickly, I needed to get up. Then, everything stopped...

Georgia Marriott (11)
Colne Valley High School, Linthwaite

The Search

After several hours of searching, a large deer caught my eye. *Thud!* went my heart as the deer munched on the leaves. Not blinking in case I missed anything, I started to make my move. My eyes watered because they were open so wide. Not wanting to give the game away, I held my breath and prowled towards the deer. All of a sudden, my heart dropped to the bottom of my stomach. *Crack!* The elegant stag shot off like a bullet and I let out my breath. I looked under my foot to see the broken twig...

Ellie Dumbrell (12)
Colne Valley High School, Linthwaite

Escape The Aliens

The chase was on, the green, slimy monsters were right behind me. I hid behind a stump but the UFO spotted me with their lights. They saw me and instantly ran towards me. My foot was stuck and they were getting closer and closer. I finally broke free and ran for my life, just making it away in time. I ran and ran and ran. I was trying my best to forget that there were hideous slimy monsters chasing after me, trying to kill me. I couldn't hear them so I turned around, but they pounced, tearing me apart...

Evan Hood (11)

Colne Valley High School, Linthwaite

Don't Find Kyla

The footsteps started... No one could find us, so I grabbed Kyla and ran, I didn't know where, I just knew they would take Kyla. Then, I came to a cliff's edge. I was trapped. I told Kyla that Daddy had to go and made the hardest decision I'd ever made. I gave Kyla a toy and told her there was a pink bird. Then, when she looked away, I ran. She screamed for me to come back. I didn't listen. Then, I heard the footsteps getting louder and louder, so I stopped. That was when I heard the bang...

Emma Cronie (11)
Colne Valley High School, Linthwaite

I Got Away

I wouldn't last much longer running, everything got smaller and it all started moving. Suddenly, the silence broke. The branches broke as it started moving closer and closer. Then, it stopped and it peered its eyes on mine. Its mouth slowly opened as it carefully crept towards me. I had a gun, but I was still in shock from seeing it rip the guts out of my partner. My arms shook with a weapon in my hands. I had a clear shot but I couldn't bring it upon myself to shoot the animal. I had to leave, now!

Sumayah Naamane (12)

Colne Valley High School, Linthwaite

The Child

Suddenly, he was running. The darkness surrounded him. He ran as guns shot. he stood still, panting. As quick as a flash, a man shouted, "Come back here you rat!" The child ran to a cave that had long vines that dangled from the top. The man who had a rifle in his hand ran past the run-down cave. He nibbled on his loaf of bread that he'd stolen from the man. A couple of hours later, he walked out of the run-down cave. The golden ball rose as the little child realised he was alone, all alone...

Lucian Howarth (12)
Colne Valley High School, Linthwaite

The Beast That Was A Tree

Not looking where I was going, I ran into a tree, Branches swung out of the ground to attack me. I ran again. Little did I know that the tree was following me. Then, I heard something like a branch swing past me. Up ahead, I saw an abandoned fairground with the lights flickering in the distance. Finally, I managed to get into the creepy place as quickly as I could. I hid under a haunted house, still and quiet, I didn't make a peep. The giant beast came and tore down the door and destroyed the fairground...

Ben Sharpe (11)
Colne Valley High School, Linthwaite

Chased

The thunder roared like a lion. I ran across the muddy, damp grass that was trying to swallow me. Jack ran beside me. He seemed pretty calm. I already thought he was a psychopath. Last week, he tried to poison our boring old teacher, Mr Richards. I think he got the idea from the Teacup Prisoner who'd been in the news lately.

After what felt like hours of running, I made a big mistake; I turned around. A man in a yellow jacket stared back and I kept running. Then, I felt a cold hand on my shoulder...

Archie Fisher (11)

Colne Valley High School, Linthwaite

Hunted

Lightning struck, I couldn't run for much longer. They were creeping closer by the second as I slowed. My legs were aching and they were going to give way any time soon. The rain poured down and the thunder roared. My clothes were soaked as if I had jumped into a swimming pool. I ran and ran and ran but then tripped over a rock. I scrambled back to my feet, this lost me time, lots of time. Warm breaths brushed the back of my neck, they were close, really close. Then, I felt a tug on my shoulder...

Olly Douglas Lodge (12)

Colne Valley High School, Linthwaite

On The Run

Panting for breath, I sprinted across the overgrown garden. My heart pumped and I felt like it would burst out of my chest. I only had twenty-four hours before he would find me and kill me with no hesitation. Carefully, I placed myself below a vast tree. It was warm but at least I had somewhere to sit and cool down for a while. A few minutes later, I somehow had the effort to drag myself up from the floor. As soon as I got up, my legs collapsed once again. Unending shivers ran down my spine rapidly...

Evie Evans (11)
Colne Valley High School, Linthwaite

Hunted!

Footsteps were coming towards the roof. The wooden trapdoor bounced. I had to go. I turned and ran to the door that led to the cottage miles away as the trapdoor opened. I ran for my life and I wasn't overexaggerating. I heard a thump behind me. The trap had been set. I jumped down the gap in the floor to splash into the pool next to the cottage. After coming back up to the surface, I was met by three men swimming towards me. I turned in panic, then closed my eyes. They came closer as I swam away...

Georgia Atherton-Quinn (12)
Colne Valley High School, Linthwaite

Following, You

I hid in the wardrobe. What a stupid thing to do. It was the first place he looked, the door's twisted knob creaked and the door opened. My body stiffened. I tried to clamber and sneak out of the wardrobe, but it was too late. *Tip tap!* Footsteps advanced towards my room. I scrambled underneath the bed. I shut my eyes so tightly, it felt like pools of acid were burning into me. When I eventually opened my eyes, in front of me was my hunter, the one with the deep yellow eyes. Then, I died...

Hettie Coleman (11)
Colne Valley High School, Linthwaite

The Night The Diary Opened Back Again

It had to be somewhere, the infamous diary that held his soul. The person who was my friend. The person my parents locked away forever. I was running through their warehouse, looking for the old floorboard. I was beginning to think it was gone, but then I tripped. The floorboard flew into the air and landed next to me. I took a look under the floor and there it was, as clear as day. As I walked up to the diary, it began to flicker. It then exploded and in the corner was a shadow. He was back...

Molly McManus (13)
Colne Valley High School, Linthwaite

Running

I couldn't run for much longer. There were thousands of them all different shapes and sizes, all hiding, ready to jump out at me. I couldn't carry on much longer. My heart was thumping so quickly, I was so scared knowing that something or someone was going to jump out at me. I carried on running. I felt like I wasn't getting anywhere. Just a matter of time now. All I wanted to do was go home and act like this never happened. As I carried on running, the forest went up in flames...

Macey Stephenson (11)
Colne Valley High School, Linthwaite

Captured

I could see the light flashing. The trees encroached over my head, blocking the rain. I stood up, my heart pounding as I began to run. They couldn't catch me, not now. I felt the wet leaves under my feet slide as I ran faster and finally, I reached the pond. The ice cracked as I tiptoed across it. I reached the other side and sat on the grass. For the first time in twelve years, I was out. I felt freedom. Then, I heard a noise. I had to leave, right now, before they found and killed me...

Edan Johnson (11)
Colne Valley High School, Linthwaite

Christmas Mayhem

It was Christmas Day once again and I was enjoying a chocolate bar by the fire when it dawned on me, it hit my brain like a brick, I had one job! I'd lost the evil pearl and I needed to get it to the Queen in a week! I got out of my chair so quickly I nearly fell over.

Finally, after a week of searching, the day had come and I still hadn't found it. I wandered awkwardly up to the Queen and she put her hand out expectantly. I twiddled my thumbs and began to explain myself...

Phoebe Searle (12)
Colne Valley High School, Linthwaite

The Hunt

The furious monster ran after me. I hid behind a stone bar. It stopped. The monster looked around like an owl, then it saw me. I froze like I was an ice sculpture. Then, the huge, furious monster slowly walked to me. I ran into the forgotten woods, running in and out of trees but I just ended up hitting all the branches. The trees whacked me in the face. The monster was the same size as a building, it was about to get me, but a bigger monster came and ate it. Then, I quickly ran away...

Cody Christopher (11)
Colne Valley High School, Linthwaite

Hunted, What Shall I Do?

It was 12:30pm when I was taking a walk through the wood. I could sense someone coming for me. My heart pounded and I began to run and out of the corner of my eye, I saw the huntsman. He was coming for me. He sounded his horn and galloped towards me. I ran faster and faster, trying to find a place to hide. I couldn't run for much longer, but then I found an old hut. Quickly, I ran inside to try and hide and sat down silently. I took a breath and sighed. I was finally free again...

Ruby Wood (11)
Colne Valley High School, Linthwaite

Predator 0.5

I woke up in a jungle, but it wasn't the type of jungle you'd find. It was an isolated jungle, but I wasn't alone. There were others coming towards me. I quickly climbed a tree, they had big, long machetes. I looked at my hands, they were bloody but at least I had some bandages. I had twenty-four hours to kill the three of them but I knew I couldn't. They were together like a pack of wolves. I knew I had to split them up, so I came up with some traps and set them around the jungle...

Jack Butterfield (11)
Colne Valley High School, Linthwaite

Running

I couldn't run for much longer. I had just escaped from prison. Okay, let me start from the beginning. I had just gone to court after someone had accused me of my wife's suicide. Now here I was, running for my life, being hunted and probably about to be shot. I was a nervous wreck. I couldn't breathe. My heart was pounding out of my chest. Where was I going to go? I had no family. I was going to die out here all alone. I felt so sick, I knew it... All of a sudden, *bang!*

Lily Haigh (11)
Colne Valley High School, Linthwaite

Hunted

Walking through the woods at 1:30pm with my friends, Emma and Jessica, we suddenly spotted a house that looked like it was haunted. It was old and a bit broken. We all decided on whether we should go in it, but we all decided to go in. As we entered the haunted house, we walked through the giant brown doors. It felt like my heart was beating out of my chest. We looked around for a bit, then we went into a room. As soon as we went into the room, someone else came in with a gun...

Grace Hirst (11)
Colne Valley High School, Linthwaite

Cheetah

I couldn't run for much longer because they were after me with their arrows as sharp as knives. About to hit me, I had to run as quickly as I could. But they were getting closer and closer. I couldn't run, I had to stop and hide behind a tree. They rode past me on their horses as fast as lightning, not seeing me. I ran back to my cave as they foolishly passed me, though I thought they'd heard me because I looked back and saw them come after me. I luckily made it back in time...

Demi Hall (11)
Colne Valley High School, Linthwaite

They Are Coming For Me!

I couldn't run for much longer. My legs were aching. I had twenty-four hours to hide or I would be gone forever. I had been running for hours. We were so close, but then I heard a bang. It hit my friend, but I had to carry on. I still had nightmares about it, how I just left him. I heard the sirens wailing behind me, but I carried on running. I had no choice, it wasn't safe now they knew I was wanted too. I had to hide right away. I hated being a wanted, lonely human.

Eva-Marie Duncan (11)
Colne Valley High School, Linthwaite

Captured...

It tried to get me, but it didn't. The wind was howling, the rain was pouring. There was no going back, it was too late. All I could hear was her lifeless voice screaming for me. My body was shaking, my heart was pounding. I didn't know what to do, but there was still no going back. I ran and ran until I could no longer. It was getting late so I got some rest, but I was in the woods so I camped out. All of a sudden, I heard a crunch and a scream. I was gone...

Evangeline Short (11)
Colne Valley High School, Linthwaite

Hunted

I couldn't run much longer, my entire body hurt and all because some human wanted to kill and stuff me to hang on his wall. *Snap!* I heard him getting closer. I ran faster and faster. *Bang!* The bullet hit my skin and pierced my stomach. I lay there dying. There was no point in running or trying to. I was weak. He was going to catch, kill and then stuff me as one of his prized possessions. I started to get sleepy as I started to fade. Then, I was dead.

Jessie Stanley-Smith (12)
Colne Valley High School, Linthwaite

Captured

I ran as fast as I could. I knew all eyes were on me, trying to catch me, trying to hunt me down. I ran as fast as I could. I couldn't let them catch me. My life depended on not getting caught. My life depended on running and not being caught. I ran through their legs. I got away, but he was still haunting me. It was like hell. My legs collapsed. I couldn't run anymore. I let them take me away. He took me. Since then, I had been trapped in my own nightmare...

Layla Parson (11)
Colne Valley High School, Linthwaite

Infectious Hunt

King Hing Ho had a furry pet cat and wondered why he was so ill. He was so posh and intimidated personnel from the army. He saw that his cat's teeth were as sharp as a knife and that its fleas were so deadly. That was what was causing the population to drop! He was soon alone, no one to go out with, no one at all. He knew the plague had finally come back to haunt him again. He was aghast. The posh people died first, then the poor until no one else was alive...

Harley Chambers (11)
Colne Valley High School, Linthwaite

Ran For My Life

John and I ran through the dense forest, diving and ducking.
Where would we run? Where would we hide? We didn't
know if we would live. John had a young family, all I had was
a mother. I had a deep anger in my soul. I ran as quick as
the wind. I shouted to John, "Run!"
We ran and ran until we got away from the hunters. We ran
to our families. I did not want to die, my mother wasn't
dead. We had to get home. We needed our families!

Jack Edwards (12)
Colne Valley High School, Linthwaite

Clown Man!

It was just a normal day when Jay was covering himself with beans while Rommel was tipping a caravan when suddenly, a colourful caravan came around the corner in a GT. They ran as fast as they could inside. They turned on the TV and looked at the news. The clown was on it, he'd escaped from Area 51. Suddenly, they heard a bang outside like a firework. It was the clown, so they ran to the backyard and got in their Bugatti Chiron and drove away.

Archie Broadbent-Allen (12)
Colne Valley High School, Linthwaite

Chasing Jane

There was a girl named Jane McGuigan. Jane's boyfriend was called Charlie. Charlie and his dad used to hunt animals. Without any warning, Charlie's dad committed suicide. Charlie reacted badly to it and started abusing Jane. Jane eventually left him and started a new chapter. Charlie started to stalk Jane.

A year passed and Charlie was still watching Jane, he knew everything about her. Jane's power went out, she went outside to check the fuse box. Jane saw a shadow. She got to the patio, then she saw him. Jane ran into the woods. She was officially on the run...

Sarah Neil (13)
Coltness High School, Coltness

The Money Man

"The suspense is killing me!" I shouted whilst waiting to see the result. At that moment, the broadcaster came on to announce the four lucky numbers. I rummaged for my ticket, it was in my pocket. I heard the four numbers... I'd won, I'd really won! Within days, friends, family, strangers I'd never met before, all stood at my front door. People were shouting, ranting. I knew they weren't here to see me, they were here for my money. Outbursts followed on the news, I felt like I was being hunted not for who I was, but for my money...

Callum Steele (14)
Coltness High School, Coltness

Don't Go Out Alone

At 12:02pm, Maria Rudenburg went missing. She was last seen in the Farmwatt shopping centre, Alabama. There was a suspicious man lurking around the shop. People in the mall awoke from their in-depth studies of clothes when they heard a scream. Heads turned as security rushed towards the exit she was taken out of. There was no sign of Maria or the man. Traffic was high, echoes of children crying were making it harder to find Maria. Nine hours of looking for her went by. She would be classed as a missing person. We were officially on the hunt...

Rhyan Czarnocki (14)
Coltness High School, Coltness

A Life For A Life

Mohammed screamed as the knife was pulled from his chest, knife scraping against bone, left to die by his partner. Traw showed no remorse as he climbed the lighting gantry to observe his work. Ten seconds later, his blond hair was lit up by a giant fireball and satisfied, he quietly left the building. Face covered, he mingled with the crowd, trying to avoid police and doing well. However, as he turned the corner, he found himself looking down the barrel of a gun. Quickly, he tried to bring up his own, but he was too slow. The officer fired.

Robbie Nicol (14)
Coltness High School, Coltness

An Escapee In The Motherland

Unfortunately, word got around the village that my family were anti-soviet. The Red Army rounded everyone up and they grabbed me. The officer unleashed his Tokarev TT33, loaded it and pointed it at me. I shoved him and ran towards the woods. The thick snow was a massive hindrance.

I'd been on the run for weeks. I could hear the army attempting to kill me, but I escaped and found a new location. This time was different, I saw probably an entire platoon of soldiers with rifles. A bullet hit me and I hit the vast, thick snow...

Ryan Nugent (14)
Coltness High School, Coltness

My Escape

As I ran, my stomach groaned louder. I needed something in my system. I ran, looking for something to eat. I'd not eaten in weeks, my bones were so brittle. Snow covered the floor. I couldn't see the twigs and stones on the ground - that worried me. Bullets were shot, but I hadn't seen any animals. I questioned what they were shooting or what they were looking for, was it me? I hadn't been paying attention to the floor. I couldn't walk. My right leg felt paralysed. I was stuck. I could hear them coming. I couldn't escape. I froze.

Emma Bett (13)
Coltness High School, Coltness

In The Shadows

Jet-black shadows covered the visibility of the men. Two were stocky in build, the other small and twig-like. They moved quickly but not into a run or jog. Across the road, they saw their prey. The sky was black like the shadows. They stood metres away from the man. The smaller of the three broke into a sprint and reached into his pocket, pulling something out, something small and shiny in the hands of its owner. The single man turned around. The aggressor drove the object through the victim's abdomen. He screamed out for help...

Cameron Pringle (13)
Coltness High School, Coltness

Gone!

There was a woman who had escaped a maximum-security prison. She was a very dangerous woman. She was being hunted down by the police but nobody could find her. The police had been looking for days, but were getting nowhere. The police started searching in the woods near the prison but so far had no luck. Nobody could see her. It was then days until suddenly, a policeman noticed a shadow lurking in the woods. They walked closer, trying not to alarm them. They got so close when the shadow ran for their life and disappeared forever.

Leah Trainor (14)
Coltness High School, Coltness

Suspicion

I no longer feel safe. I have this regular, Jack's his name, or so he said. The rest of us stay away, get a weird vibe. Can't blame them, but needs must. We'd met before, he was angry, said there was something he had to do. That same night, Ms Eddowes and Ms Stride's bodies were found. I try not to accuse, but this seems too obvious. I'm going to mention something tonight. Although if I meet one's death, just remember, my name is Mary Jane Kelly and I believe I may be the next victim of Jack the Ripper...

Reis Millar (14)
Coltness High School, Coltness

Shoplifter

As I was out shopping, I noticed that the woman beside me sneaked Airpods into her pocket. When I realised what she'd just done, she was off. I quickly alerted security. They spoke through their radios. They got her. I decided to follow them to see what was going to happen. As the woman tried to leave the mall, security ran faster. When the woman got outside, she jumped into a stolen vehicle and dashed off. Then, I saw the police arrest her. As I went into Apple to continue shopping, they rewarded me with a free iPhone 11 Pro.

Skylar Quigley (14)
Coltness High School, Coltness

The Bright Pink Ogre

Oggie the bright pink ogre struggled to make friends because of her massive nose that she used to hunt for cocoa powder. The cocoa powder was used to make marshmallow hot chocolate. Oggie smelled cocoa powder as she turned around, there was a monster ready to eat her! Oggie was being hunted, she had nowhere to go and nobody to help her. Oggie saw a tree house that she could use for safety. A big, pink, fluffy marshmallow welcomed her. He opened his puffy arms for a hug and, for the first time in Oggie's life, she felt loved.

Lara Houston (13)
Coltness High School, Coltness

Argentina Manhunt

Me and José had been ghosted for several months now and time was running out. The feds were closing in on us. We would probably have another week. Then, we'd be done. We packed up and retreated to the jungle many miles away. The dark canopy overhead kept us undercover.

After a week of hiding, we heard shouting from a distance. This could be the end. I woke José silently. He rose, groaning. My hand shot to his mouth. I told him we were leaving. A bang and a flash blinded me. José's body dropped. I dropped with it...

Dylan King (14)
Coltness High School, Coltness

Wrongly Accused

I had twenty-four hours to get out of here for good and never come back. I was getting hunted by what felt like everyone for something I didn't do. You're probably wondering what was going on. To cut a long story short, I was in the wrong place at the wrong time and got accused of killing three politicians. I'm currently hiding in my auntie's loft, but I have to get a bus or something out of London, fast. I decide to leave when I hear a massive bang on the door. "Open up! It's the police!"

Lucy Smith (14)
Coltness High School, Coltness

On The Run

I was being chased down like a dog, more like hunted. These new marshalls aren't giving up. Me and Petey had been running for a while now. I should never have trusted that Josiah! It was him that was supposed to keep the hostages in check. We heard the clattering of horses clammer on the earth. My revolver cocked and ready, Petey fired. I quickly went through my gun's capacity. I turned to run but that was when I realised all those people were people we'd robbed. The job wasn't supposed to be that difficult...

Kalib Blair (14)
Coltness High School, Coltness

Left For Dead

My heart was racing. Where was I? I was lost. That was when I realised what had happened. I saw a shadow come towards me, at this point my heart almost shot out of my chest. I ran. The man began chasing me. I ran as fast as I could, but I couldn't seem to get away. I heard branches cracking in my direction. Then I felt hands around my neck... I woke up. I heard sirens. Who could've called them? I was taken to the hospital and was greeted by someone saying, "I didn't mean it..."

Reece Hooper (14)
Coltness High School, Coltness

Silence Of The Forest

Gunshot after gunshot. I was hiding behind a tree. It was completely silent. My heartbeat was ringing in my ears. I jolted my head up to the noise of leaves crunching. The noise was coming closer and I didn't know what to do. I took a deep breath and made a run for it. I put one foot in front of the other as fast as possible. I heard him running behind me. I tripped over a branch. *Bang!* Then silence. I sat up in shock. His body was in front of me. The last thing I heard was sirens...

Erin Joan MacGregor (14)
Coltness High School, Coltness

Stalked

I'm at the house watching TV, there have been noises all
night. It's late, so I decide to go to bed. On my way, I hear
clicks but shrug them off. I wake up the next morning
remembering last night, but am snapped out of it by the
same clicking. I try looking for the source of the noise, but I
can't find it. I ignore it but at night, I can't anymore. I get
thirsty so decide to go to the kitchen. On my way, I hear the
same click. Then a flash. I soon realise I'm being stalked...

Abby Clarke (14)
Coltness High School, Coltness

Hiding In The Shadows

One night, I was out walking my dog and I let her off the leash. I noticed that she ran away, so I looked for her. I found her hanging from a tree, dead. I let out a horrific, blood-curdling scream and started running. I felt something grab my wrist and pull me back. I screamed more and more. The killer tied me to a tree. She told me that, if I didn't stop, she'd kill me. I screamed more, she got a sharp knife. Then, she stabbed me in the stomach, causing a slow, painful death...

Grace Galloway (13)
Coltness High School, Coltness

Pay Day

We were close. Everyone was uneasy about the job but we still got on with it. We were outside the bank. As soon as we got in the bank, the police surrounded it. Obviously someone talked but we didn't know who. We couldn't get anything because we were all worrying about not getting caught. One of us surrendered and three of us went out the back entrance. But we had no car so we ran as fast as we could. When we found a car, the police were on our tails. We went down a road... That was it.

Nathan Rodgers (13)
Coltness High School, Coltness

My Life Changed Forever

Today, my life changed forever. It was Halloween, I was out trick or treating when it was discovered that I had robbed an old lady's shop. I didn't know the boys chasing after me screaming, "Stop!" One of the boys was her grandson. I was panicking, they were going to kill me. I was running, running. I fell over a broken branch. I tried to get up as fast as I could when I saw a wolf coming towards me. The group of boys stopped. I got up only to fall down a hole...

Hollie Macnamara (13)
Coltness High School, Coltness

Obsession

I was on the beach now, trapped. Hoping he wouldn't come here. When we were younger, we used to visit here all the time. I knew he hated it, but he would come just for me. It got to the point where he was never not with me. He was obsessed. It was my first love and it was a beautiful feeling until it ended. I didn't know if it was for him hearing, "I don't love you anymore," that made him want revenge or that he was an insane person. Had I been caught now after all this time...?

Jane Macmillan (14)
Coltness High School, Coltness

Breathing

All of a sudden, I felt a cold breeze down my spine like someone was breathing down my neck. I shivered uncontrollably. I couldn't stop, but then all of a sudden, I heard something. I tried to imagine what it was but it was so quiet it was hard to hear well enough. It slowed and I thought it was footsteps. Then they got louder and louder until it was horrifyingly loud. It was spine-chilling. I didn't know what was going on, but I knew it wasn't good. Then, it went quiet...

Sean Allen (13)
Coltness High School, Coltness

The Escaped

I was hidden but I knew I couldn't stay for long. I couldn't feel anything. That... prison, that was no normal prison. They made me forget my name, how old I was and they shaved my head. The sirens wailed and the red and blue lights shone through the trees. I knew I couldn't get away, they would chase me until they found me. The trees were good as cover to hide and go from place to place. I had no idea where to go, no idea where to hide. I ran across the road...

Jamie Roddie (13)
Coltness High School, Coltness

Lodge In The Forest

I couldn't run for much longer. I was in a state of panic. September 25th, 1981, I was running from my hunter. I had miles to go to the nearest town. I was running out of breath. I had a trickle of water left and $5 in my pocket to survive. If you're wondering what on Earth is going on, I was staying in a lodge and a huntsman broke in. He wanted to kill me. He held me by the neck, told me to be quiet or I would be shot. He turned for a minute and I ran.

Ayley Crawford (14)
Coltness High School, Coltness

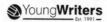

The Hole

My head was aching, it felt like I had been running for ages. It could have been days, minutes or hours. It had been dark for as long as I could remember. I was being chased by one of the most hideous creatures I had ever seen. My mum had always told me, if I was being chased by someone or something, I should just run, so I did. I heard something behind me so I ran as fast as I could until I fell down a hole. I thought I was dead until I woke up in my bed.

Abigail Craig (13)
Coltness High School, Coltness

Stranger Danger

Sam's the most gorgeous guy on Earth. We met via Instagram. He looks like a model. He wants to know me, but I don't think I'm pretty.

Earlier, he messaged me. He's in town and wants to meet up outside the library. My parents think I'm shopping with friends. They wouldn't approve of boyfriends, especially ones two years older and ones I haven't met yet.

Approaching the library, I see only an old man. I hear tyres screeching alongside me. As I turn, a door opens and the old man pushes me in. "Hello Skye, I'm Sam..."

Skye Elizabeth Myers Burney (11)
Dean Trust Rose Bridge, Ince-In-Makerfield

That Night

It was a dark night when I was on my way home through the forest. Then, I heard it. I started to run but it was behind me. This time, I heard multiple howls. There were more of them. They started to chase me. I hurt myself getting away through bushes and past branches.

When I got out of the forest, they chased me through the streets and almost caught me. People watched in horror. The wolves stopped, looking me dead in the eyes. They growled and turned away, leaving me bleeding, crying and hurting. Painfully, I went home...

Simon Doodson-Smith (14)

Dean Trust Rose Bridge, Ince-In-Makerfield

The Pain Within Me

I woke up paralysed. It had happened again, the dreams, the fear, the drowning. I had known that in my past life, I was a witch. I was Bridget Bishop, the first person to be executed for witchcraft during the Salem Witch Trials in 1692. 200 were tried, eighteen others were executed, fourteen women and five men. I lived in fear they would come for me, see the mark of the witch and I'd be discovered again. I was or I could be again, given the chance, the strongest, most powerful witch... She would rise again.

Amelia Southall (11)
Dean Trust Rose Bridge, Ince-In-Makerfield

Found You

"Nine, ten..." I didn't know where to hide. I quickly hid in the closet. All I could hear was, "Ready or not, here I come!" There was another boy playing, Jack. I knew I was going to lose this... "Found you!" Jack was caught. I sat inside the closet, knowing I wouldn't be found for a while. I heard the boys laughing and I got nervous and stood back up. One of them said, "I bet he's in the closet." I hid behind the clothes in the closet. They walked into the room and opened the closet door... "Found you!"

Kaitlyn Cox (11)
Dean Trust Rose Bridge, Ince-In-Makerfield

It's Coming...

If you are reading this, I am dead. I've had this lingering feeling for a long time. I've heard stories, but I didn't listen. I don't know how I got here, bodies everywhere. I feel sick. It's close. You can feel it, like when you wake up at night and you sense you're being watched. You don't feel it here, you know it. You are being watched and then it's too late. I'm dead and I won't be able to warn you. There is no hope for me, but you, you are able to run. Run now!

Sam Simmons (15)
Homewood College, Brighton

Tears

Tears. Streaming down my face, like a river, never-ending, constantly flowing. My eyes black, bruised, swollen. Laughing. They sniggered at me as I ran from the crowd. Jenna stood there, watching me run, laughing at the way my clothes are ripped and that blood is seeping from the gash across my foot. I went down a narrow alley, hoping the herd of girls didn't see me slip away. Suddenly, I saw a shadow approaching from the footpath. Jenna, followed by her coven of ravenous, vile witches, cornered me into the dusty crevice of the alley. They all smirked...

Lacey Harwood (12)
Onslow St Audrey's School, Hatfield

Burnt In Hell

Fire blazed, corrupting years of work. I breathed rapidly, eyes hooked on a burning monstrosity. Children's screams filled the house. *I'd better go or they'll catch me*, I thought worryingly. Officers ran, gaining speed quickly. I jumped up, frightened, releasing my legs. I took off into the night at the speed of light. My adrenaline rushed through me, taking control. Dogs viciously barked in search of prey. Regret filled me how I'd ruined their day. Suddenly, I stopped. They were here. Dogs tugged, ripping my clothes, tearing my limbs. Busted. Behind bars, left there to die for all eternity...

Riley Shaw (11)
Ryde Academy, Ryde

Help Me, I'm Perfectly Fine

They wail and shriek, expressing the oxymoronic vapid rage of grief. They pound on the soft ground. They spear, stab and impale each other, but the screaming won't stop. Disembowelment, consummation. The screaming won't stop. It just won't. They are invisible to the eye, but I can't stop seeing them. They crawl and skitter, nails dig and tear, tear almost as deep as the screaming. They disappear and sleep, resting for another session of vicious laceration. Clawing, punching, smacking at themselves, at me. Screaming, they see me just as much as I see them. Killing me from the inside out...

Callum Winter (12)
Ryde Academy, Ryde

They Mustn't Know

It's happened again, every night now. I can't stop it. He won't stop pushing me for answers of her death. I plead, "Brother, this isn't you, stop!" He doesn't listen. He can't hear me from down there.

Gasping for breath, I awaken, back aching in pain. My spinal cord ripped from me, as well as my heels. I hear a faint squeak, whimpering. I turn my head: my sister is standing there with her mouth open, her eyes wide. I've failed. I promised they wouldn't know, wouldn't know what I was becoming. They had to go. I'd promised him...

Scarlett de Havilland (13)
Ryde Academy, Ryde

Skeleton Hands

He had been running, hunted by her. Seven days of constant torture, he had to stop. Exhausted and suffering from frostbite, he sat down on the icy ground. In the distance came the sweet humming of an engine. They were here. They had found him, but how? His heart raced. His chest tightened. His palms were sweaty. Adrenaline pulsed through the bulging veins on the side of his sweat-stricken face. He ran, but for how long could he last? The frozen wasteland flashed past. The trees' skeleton hands reached out, capturing the graceful snowflakes in their deadly embrace...

Evie Thomas (12)
Ryde Academy, Ryde

Demonic Cravings

"We have to leave, now," I said. But here I am on the run, abandoning my friends so I can possibly live another day. I can remember the howls and wails of the cannibalistic predators as they gave chase.

Shaking my head, bringing myself back to the present proves difficult. A quiet eerieness suddenly envelops the surrounding woods. Through the low-lying mist, I see a dishevelled cabin. Refuge... Once inside, exhaustion overcomes me and I sleep to be woken by a wetness on my face and harrowing yellow eyes. Fear strikes, my breathing heightened...

Ella Crowther (13)
Ryde Academy, Ryde

On The Run

"It has to be here somewhere, we've been looking for a long time now..."
The suspense grew, the siren wailed amongst the dark forest. We couldn't lose it because the police would find out who had stolen it. We had been looking all day and we still hadn't found it. It would be hard to find it because it was so small. We heard running throughout the forest and had to hide. The police walked past us but luckily they weren't convinced anyone was there. We didn't think anyone was there but there was... We were caught by them!

Emma Noble (13)
Ryde Academy, Ryde

Hunted

I couldn't run for much longer, they were after me. The acid rain was hammering down onto my bare skin, the sound of the sirens was deafening. The hunt had commenced, they weren't going to give up. They kept getting closer and closer. I was approaching many turnings, which one was I going to take? The fear and worry inside me was my campaign to keep going. The smell of human blood filled my nostrils. I turned to see where they were, closer than I anticipated! I could just make out the towering, extensive figure, blood dripping from its mouth...

Alesha Roberts (13)
Ryde Academy, Ryde

Run

"It has to be here somewhere!" They searched the desolate interior of the house.
"Where could it be, there aren't many places it could be!" one of them exclaimed.
"Bingo! We need to leave, time is running out for us to escape them."
They all exited promptly. She stopped, observing the strange setting she had ended up in.
"Hey! Come on, we don't have time to run, run!" She knew there wasn't time, but everything around her was spinning. She just needed a moment where time would stop. She still kept on running, they kept on running.

Becca Aspden (13)
Ryde Academy, Ryde

The Lost

They were coming, as fast as lightning. I decided to keep going. The snow I stood on crumpled into lots of pieces. Mystically, the icy wind breathed down my neck. The trees covered themselves with snow, hiding themselves from what was coming. I looked back, they were still coming, menacing looks in their eyes. Snowflakes slowly danced their enchanted dance to land on the soft cushion of snow. Underneath that snow would be where I'd be left if I gave up now. The woods were the only possibility. I looked behind me, they weren't going to give up...

Ben Moralee (12)
Ryde Academy, Ryde

The Mystery

It had to be here somewhere. I couldn't leave it here... *Bang!*
I jumped out of my wardrobe, my sister struggling up the
creaky stairs. Screaming violently, she tripped and fell into
my arms. She was too afraid to tell me what it was, her
tears turned into a waterfall! The mystery stomped up the
stairs slowly but aggressively. It had to be here somewhere!
But we had to find safety. I pushed my sister under my bed
whilst running to my wardrobe, frightened. This would have
to be such a traumatic experience for my six-year-old
sister...

Bam Ruth
Ryde Academy, Ryde

Surrounded

It had to be here somewhere. I ran into the next room, panic rising in me. Outside, the enemy surrounded the crumbling building, yelling over the top of the helicopter's roars. *Don't think of who they were, think of what they are now. Blank them out. Keep looking.* The drawers were empty, the bed broken, the cupboard in pieces. The next room, more yells. A loud explosion and old wood flew across the corridor. It had better be in here, otherwise, it'd be over. Shouts. Footsteps. They were coming for me. It was under the bed. The gun...

Danny Wilson (14)
Ryde Academy, Ryde

The Hunt

I still have nightmares about it, the infection had swiftly spread across the globe, corrupting everyone it came in contact with. Several months ago, the military had abolished the threat, but it still felt like it was still there. Sometimes, it felt like it was still there inside me. Every day, I ran further from civilisation, hoping they'd given up. Before I left the city, the others had found out about my condition and then, so did the police. A bounty was set on me so I wouldn't be a threat. My condition was unstable and I was worried...

Rhys Mundell (14)
Ryde Academy, Ryde

Hunted

It has to be here somewhere. I need it, the key to the back door. "It's him," I whisper to myself. The hunter. I look in Mum's old drawers and hear a bang. He's breaking down the door. I grab the key out the drawer, the key works! I fling the door open and bolt towards the woods. I've never been this petrified in my life.

After an hour of running, I find a hut. It's raining so I don't hesitate one bit before entering. He's in there, waiting for me. "Hello, I've been expecting you..."

Taya Cotton (11)
Ryde Academy, Ryde

Hunting In Silence

"It's not safe, they can't know." I woke up to those words.
They were talking about me. This very day was the
beginning of the hunt. The day started normal, I had eaten
my food, people were walking past my cell, whispering,
trying to stay as far away as possible.

Later, it was time... They ran terrified, wearing body armour,
armed with the sharpest swords. They covered my eyes and
locked me up. Minutes later, they dragged me out. The
sirens went. The hunt in silence had begun. I was ready to
hunt and so it began...

Caitlin Jessica John (12)
Ryde Academy, Ryde

Escape

The sirens wailed in my ears. It had been two hours straight of non-stop running. It was over. After years of successful business, I left this land empty-handed. The others had betrayed me and now I found myself running. I didn't know why. Suddenly, silence surrounded me just like the police. In the corner of my weary eye, I spotted a lake. Should I risk it? The police were caught by surprise as I leapt onto the frozen lake. Unfortunately, the ice snapped into tiny pieces and I fell through. There was no hope of survival... or was there?

Sara Setzu (12)
Ryde Academy, Ryde

When Darkness Takes Over

I run through the dark ditches and forests, trying to find my prey. I hear my fellow hunters rustling through the trees. The sirens wail, the dogs howl as we go on through the night. I can feel the vibrations rumble through the ground then rattle through me. I can see bright luminous lights shining in the distance while also lighting up the night sky. The dog force is searching for the getaway drivers, but we don't get much luck. It goes silent. I hear a rustle behind me. I turn. Suddenly, everything is turned off. Darkness takes over...

Kayleigh Batchelor (14)
Ryde Academy, Ryde

Hunted By The Snow Foxes

The winter breeze blew through my fur. It ran through the thick snow. They were coming, the foxes. The rabbit's legs were freezing cold and it had to go a little further. It ran down the hill, making a mistake by looking back. There was a group of bundles of fluff, but they were devils. The worst thing about them was their strong jaws. *Bang!* The rabbit lay on the soft snow and the foxes approached. They stopped in their tracks and then ran. The little, frightened rabbit looked up and saw a beautiful red fox wagging his tail.

Erica Roberts (13)
Ryde Academy, Ryde

The Escapist

As I scaled the tall, chequered metal fence, the small number of guards (due to the fact that Operation Barbarossa was in full swing) were about to start their patrol. I didn't have long. I climbed the fence and hopped over the barbed wire below. From now, I had minutes to get away as far as I could. After only minutes, I heard the sirens boom. The sheer sound almost knocked me off my feet. They were coming. They would have guard dogs sniffing for my scent. Lights brightened through every inch of the dark woods. I wasn't safe...

George Hiorns (12)
Ryde Academy, Ryde

The Bike

One day, a boy called Tim decided to go into the woods. As the sun went down, Tim didn't realise the time because he was practising his tricks on his bike. Because he was in the shade, it made no difference to the light. Soon, a shadow came from behind him. A tall, white figure stood before him. "What are you doing around here at this time of day?" Tim said he was practising and didn't realise what time it was. Silence. There was no response from the strange figure. Tim turned around, picked up the bike and ran.

Nathan Day (13)
Ryde Academy, Ryde

Nightmare

I still have nightmares about it. Lying in the marsh-ridden ground, surrounded by an eerie silence. I was used to people screaming and crying uncontrollably, but now it was as if they'd cried so much that they couldn't shed a single tear. A blanket of grey smoke suffocated me. My head whirled around. All I could see was a flood of soldiers chasing me with deadly weapons. My mind ran away till I woke up with beads of sweat rolling down my forehead and my heart pounding out of my chest like a herd of elephants marching across Africa...

Lillie Ghetty-Evans (13)
Ryde Academy, Ryde

Fire

I was asleep, a peaceful slumber. I awoke to screams. I looked out upon my village, people frantically running, children crying. Then, I smelt it, a familiar yet dangerous smell, the smell of death and decay. I jumped, just as it burst through my door. I ran, the beast quick on my heels. It felt like death was swallowing up the world I had known for so long, my small thin legs aching with each bound, desperately trying to escape the raging creature. I tripped and stumbled, the beast inching towards me. It was fire that killed me...

Chloe Cowans (13)
Ryde Academy, Ryde

Halloween

Deep breathing came from the cupboard. She was asleep on the bed until there was a bang. She shot up with hair on the back of her neck standing up. The sirens wailed in the distance. The man appeared from his hiding spot and the woman let out an ear-piercing scream and ran for the door. Close behind her was the man. He was wearing a mechanical suit with a white, pale mask. He was holding a butcher's knife that had blood dripping off it. As she ran towards the sirens, there were multiple screams and the sirens fell silent...

Ewan Gascoigne (12)
Ryde Academy, Ryde

Running Out Of Time

I still have nightmares about that day. It all started when I was walking through the dark, gloomy forest. Ivy twisted around the paths like it was trying to trap me. I fell, hugging myself for comfort. Red eyes glared at me through the bushes. Suddenly, I found myself spinning high into the air. Sirens wailed, my heart rate increased. The taste of fear filled my mouth. I tried to get out. Untying the knot was difficult like lighting a match with ice. I heard leaves rustling and loud footsteps getting closer. Time was up...

Amelia Day (11)
Ryde Academy, Ryde

On The Run

The sirens wailed, they had found us. We weren't alone. We'd been running for days, we thought we had eluded her but obviously not. They wanted what we had, thinking it was rightfully theirs, but it wasn't. They were never going to stop until they had what they wanted. I heard footsteps behind us. "You can't get away!" she said.

We ran through the forest, we had to get away and quickly. I tripped on a tree trunk and twisted my ankle. I couldn't go on. "You're not getting away this time," she cackled. The hunt was over...

Violet Slimm (11)
Ryde Academy, Ryde

That Night

It was dark, all I could hear were dogs barking and footsteps crunching the leaves. I was tired and out of breath, but I couldn't stop. I felt them getting closer and closer. I couldn't see where I was going, but I had to run faster. The dogs were growling, the police were shouting. All of a sudden, it went silent. I could hear the wind howling in my ears. My heart pounding, I had a feeling I was caught. Suddenly, I heard a stick snap. I was down and now I still have nightmares from that dark, mysterious night...

Brooke De'ath (12)
Ryde Academy, Ryde

The Hunter

I couldn't run for much longer, the forest was gloomy and becoming deeper the more I ran. My feet were aching, my pulse was racing. Could I carry on? I could feel his presence and hear his heavy footsteps crunching on twigs. The hunted. I knew he was near, my heart was beating through my chest.

He had found me, a black silhouette stood at the end of the darkened tunnel. Running, my feet began to trip. Panting heavily, I could hear him shouting my name over and over. Then, a heavy hand gripped my shoulder...

Tilly Nicholls (13)
Ryde Academy, Ryde

Freedom

We were pushed out, forced to run. "The creatures are out here, we have to go." The problem was, I couldn't run. I recently sprained my ankle. I had to keep going, the creatures had finally caught our scent. We all started running, the only way we could get out was by having to climb the walls, but there was only one area to get out. We were cornered, the creatures slowly moving closer. There was no way out. Suddenly, one of us realised there was a rope to our right. The rope broke. This was the end...

Nathan Arnold-Recalde (13)
Ryde Academy, Ryde

The Search

I still have nightmares about it to this day. It was a winter's night and I was trying to find something, something that could damage someone for life. I was close. I was in an abandoned mansion where someone recently died from a shootout. I found the weapon under the stairs. It was very old. I was going to shoot the man who'd killed my darling mother. All of a sudden, I heard a floorboard creak. I had a look. It was him in a newly-bought suit. I pulled out the gun. *Bang!* The hunter had just been hunted...

Lloyd Nicholls (11)
Ryde Academy, Ryde

The Murders

I couldn't run for much longer. Legs burning, heart racing, I reluctantly ran on so I wouldn't get killed. I had to get out of here. I knew their secret, I saw them die. They disappeared into the abyss of the water, I couldn't help. I was framed, I couldn't outwit them. They were coming for me, I knew it. They had found me. Shouts and engines grew louder; I could see them in the distance. I had to try and outrun them. They didn't want me telling the world the truth about them. This was it...

Kacie Hodgson (12)
Ryde Academy, Ryde

Death Is Inevitable

Running, burning through the impenetrable snowy landscape with a flamethrower spitting out fiery heat. The breath of my target, one of the only signs of life on the island of Canada. I knew I had to lead him to something he couldn't pass. A frozen-over lake. He wouldn't risk it, would he? My chance was here, I heard him. Soon, we arrived at the lake. Unsurprisingly, he leapt straight onto the lake. The ice cracked and he fell through. I knew he would die. The water was cold. There was no hope. He had to die...

Leo Stone (11)
Ryde Academy, Ryde

The Experiment

We were so close, Experiment LX16 was almost a success. Now I was hunted by a beast. Why did they have to pass that no clones law? If the beast didn't get me, I was going away for good. We'd wanted to change the world, to make the next evolution of mankind. They were all dead now, everyone on my team slaughtered by the beast. It was here, I could hear it, the pounding footsteps of that vile monster. Seven-feet tall with a mouth of fangs, claws the size of my arms, coming for me with one aim: to feed...

Joseph Paice-Jones (12)
Ryde Academy, Ryde

Nightmare

I still have nightmares about it, that night my brother went missing. The flashbacks are haunting me. I remember the man that took him, what he looked like, what he sounded like, even what car he drove. I still hear the screams, I hear his voice in my mind. It's like he's in my head. I feel him by my side when I'm down or mad like he's still here. My life is much different without my brother. He was like my sibling soulmate! I call his name all the time, "Jason! Jason!" I hear him...

Grace Nicholls
Ryde Academy, Ryde

The Huntress

I am in an abandoned school. Why? Because it's the only place I can go. I'm here because a woman called The Huntress is chasing me. I have been stabbed with her sword and the legend is that, once you've been stabbed with the blade of The Huntress' sword, you will be marked and she will chase you to the ends of the Earth until you're lying on the floor, dead. I need to lie down because I'm tired, but as soon as I lie down, I see The Huntress standing outside the window, staring at me...

Violet Paxton
Ryde Academy, Ryde

I Could Not Run For Much Longer!

It was 9pm, time for my usual night walk. I closed my door and walked down the street. The woods I never feared, unlike everyone else. Tonight, that changed. It was about 9:30pm, I heard a bang, a gunshot. I wasn't phased because there was a farm close by, however, it was unusual for them to be out this late. *Bang!* Now I was scared. I started to head home but, when I turned around, I wasn't familiar with where I was. *Bang!* I ran and ran until I couldn't run for much longer... *Bang!*

Khaila Hill-Crewe (11)
Ryde Academy, Ryde

The Kiss Of Death

I couldn't run any longer. My legs felt numb. Giving way, I fell onto the sharp twigs beneath me. The cold December wind clung to my skin. I hugged my knees against my chest. Something moved in front of me, meandering through the trees. Suddenly, a tall slim figure swiftly swept in front of me. His eyes were wide and amber and, as he stared, it felt like my soul was being sucked from my body. A thick liquid poured from his mouth; he was coming closer and closer. It knelt, ready to give the kiss of death...

Emily Ainsworth (11)

Ryde Academy, Ryde

The End

I had twenty-four hours. Twenty-four hours to drive all the way to Cardiff, rob the bank and go. There was a very awkward drive with my daughter. I had to drop her off to her mum's. At the time, I was very miserable, any little noise my daughter made, I shouted, "Shut up!" The minute I dropped her off, I sped up the M5 and took out my phone and called the driver. Soon after I called him, I picked him up from a local café. I rolled up a cigarette and, when I was down, I heard a beep...

Beau Bowden (11)
Ryde Academy, Ryde

Oh No!

A few days ago, my boyfriend proposed after five years of being together. I said yes. It was lovely knowing that you'd found someone to spend the rest of your life with and to wear an amazing ring that shone in the daylight.
The other day, I was cleaning the house while my fiancé was at work. I realised my ring was gone. I searched everywhere and couldn't find it. After a while of searching, I called my mum to tell her the sad news. Then, I saw something shine in the sunlight... It was the ring!

Kelly Morgan (12)
Ryde Academy, Ryde

Blood

They were after blood. My family had lived in here for many years, but I had wandered too far. This was all my fault. Even now, I could see the Jeep's headlights blaring through the oaks. I had been hunted since I was born. There were rumours, rumours that anyone born into my family had cursed blood. Every time I looked through the treetops, it always sickened me to see the bottles of my ancestors' blood in the nearest shop. I heard a snap behind me. Needles shot out from the Jeep. I had been found...

Monika Bielik (11)
Ryde Academy, Ryde

Apocalypse

The sound of gunshots echoed beyond the trees. My heart was pounding against my chest. I felt as if it was going to burst out. I sprinted towards a bedraggled-looking cabin. The door was hanging off its hinges, but it would do. I slumped myself under the window and reached for my revolver, fear filling my body at a rapid pace. Suddenly, I felt something metal touch my head. I stiffly turned my head and standing above me was a scruffy middle-aged man holding a double-barrelled shotgun to my forehead...

Matthew Artress-Brown (13)
Ryde Academy, Ryde

Hunted!

I couldn't run for much longer, they had almost caught me, but I had just slipped away. They must be right on my tail. I continued. Soon, I came to a little shed in the middle of nowhere. I went inside to hide and kill the time, hoping the hunters didn't find me.

They had no idea where I had gone, I thought. I tried to make my movements as difficult to read as possible. I heard something outside, I tried not to make a sound. I was terrified. They burst into the shed, they had me. I was hunted...

Christopher Sillito (13)
Ryde Academy, Ryde

I Had Twenty-Four Hours

I had twenty-four hours. I didn't know how I was going to escape this monster. It was gigantic. It killed almost everyone around me. I was struggling. I couldn't run for much longer. The monster was ten paces behind me. My life depended on this; my brother was next to me, but the monster had killed him. I was alone. I started to fade. I heard sirens chasing after me. I was stuck. I didn't know if I was going to make it. All of a sudden, the damp floor met my face. My legs, exhausted, had given up...

Amalie Yardley (11)
Ryde Academy, Ryde

Catch The Light

We were close, I could see the light but needed to get there first. The hunter! I saw his silhouette up ahead backed against the lights, facing us. I felt my blood run to my head as if I were going to faint. We kept going towards the lights with a steady fog where the hunter stood. The lights went out. We stopped.

I didn't remember what had happened, but the lights came back on and I was the only one standing. Directly in front of me was the hunter. They had all been hunted and I was next...

Megan Pugmire (14)
Ryde Academy, Ryde

Hunted

Panic forced me to go deeper into the forest as I heard my teammates being shot by the hunter. I ducked under branches, snapped twigs and ran for my life. I ran out of breath and hid behind a tree. The hunter ran past me. After I had caught my breath, I sprinted towards an old shack. Inside the shack were tools that seemed to be useless...
Ten minutes later, I found a gun, but it had no ammo. Then, I saw some ammo on the shelf. I inserted it into the gun. The hunter had become the hunted...

Jacob Coates (12)
Ryde Academy, Ryde

Hunting

I saw him, the last one. I had waited long enough. I couldn't let him go again, not now, not ever. I felt blood trickle down my forehead, it was cold. He ran faster than the others, he was stronger but he was weak against me. Because of the suspense, it was silent, silent enough for me to hear him panting pathetically. Suddenly, I realised we were heading towards the mist. I could have lost him, but I couldn't. I needed to stay focused. That was when I saw him. I ran until... "Tag! Got you!"

Robyn Moody (12)
Ryde Academy, Ryde

The Wild Revenge

I was always afraid of being hunted. I was always expecting to be killed. Then, finally, I was free. Until I found my mum./ She was lying on the ground, disintegrating. I was in shock. I heard a gunshot, it kept on going off in my head. When I settled down that night, all I could think about was my mother, how much I missed her. All I wanted was her back. The thought of never seeing her again was chilling. How dare they kill my mother, my only wolf. Miss her? It was time to get my revenge...

Madison Bloomfield (12)
Ryde Academy, Ryde

The Hunted Bear

The hunters are getting closer and closer by the minute. I can feel it haunting me in my soul. I kept running for my life and the fear of getting caught is beyond me. I still remember the nightmares that haunt me when I think of my family. All of my precious possessions, my important memories, still stay in my mind every day. I put so many lives at risk that day, I can't stop thinking about it. I was only a lonely bear who wasn't brought up to be mean. I just need to keep running...

Hayley Louise Molloy (11)
Ryde Academy, Ryde

They're After Me...

They're after me... the rozzers. They can't find me, can they? Time to move. I cross the road when suddenly, a rozzer comes flying around the corner. They don't see me. I run as fast as I can to the airport fence. I reach up and pull myself over. I sprint to the plane and make my way to the runway and take off. I carry on flying until I reach the boat waiting for me. Time to jump. I open the door and jump. I deploy my parachute and land on the boat with my friend waiting for me.

Nikita Henry-Gorshanov (12)
Ryde Academy, Ryde

The Dirt Is Gone

He was furious. Barry Scott was going to kill me. The dirt was everywhere. I needed to find the golden Cillit Bang and I needed to do it fast. Otherwise, he was going to find me and he was going to kill me. I took the golden Cillit Bang, but he saw me so I darted out of the way. He was chasing me all through the forest. I realised how far away the dirt was and I decided to punch Barry Scott. His head cracked like an egg, but then he regenerated. "Bang! The dirt is gone..."

Lewis Woolven (13)
Ryde Academy, Ryde

My First Win

Running is so hard. I hear bullets going past my ears, so I build a box and put a trap on the wall. Someone breaks the wall and gets hurt by the trap. I get my golden shotgun out and kill them with it. I hear some footsteps. I sit there in silence. I hear the fox on their back making noise. There are only four more players left now. I hear a lot of fighting around me. There are only three more players left. I think they all died because of the storm... Then, I hear I'd won...

Hazel Dawn Everard (13)
Ryde Academy, Ryde

Run

My friend and I were on wanted posters everywhere. We were already fugitives, so he said, "Meet me at Hastings. I'll get a copter..."
For what felt like years, I had been hunted. A gritty layer of sweat and blood was covering me. Just three minutes until my train to Hastings was here. I heard the sirens. The sound of death that had tormented me for ages. The train was pulling up, but so was the car. I closed my eyes and leapt to the back of the train...

Isaac Turvey (12)
Ryde Academy, Ryde

Run While You Can

How did my life get to this? This was the one question I repeated over and over again. The only thing I could do was run. After a while, my body started to feel heavier. I gasped for breath. I couldn't run for much longer. It felt as if my weight doubled in the last two minutes. My life was on the line... I could hear footsteps thudding behind me. All of a sudden, I ran into something. My weak body fell backwards, knowing that this was the end. No one could save me now...

Isabelle Bull (13)
Ryde Academy, Ryde

The Hunter

We were close. We were sprinting as fast as we could. The end was so near, but so was he. Then, all I heard was screaming. I looked to my left, nobody was there. I looked to my right, nobody was there. I was all alone, just me in the forest. Alone with a psycho. I heard him running like a stallion. I tripped on a log and grazed my knees. I thought that it was over, but luckily for me, it was only my friend. They took me home, sat me down and spoke to me. I was relieved.

Preston George Groves
Ryde Academy, Ryde

The Big Chase

I had twenty-four hours. I ran down the hill and entered the forest and looked behind me. I saw the man flying towards me. I jumped into the river and tried to stay underwater to not let the man see me. After a while, the man went off to find me, but I was still there. I had twenty-three hours and forty-seven minutes left and I thought I could survive it. I thought of food and drink and went back to the river. Before I knew it, I was back in there after being stabbed...

Jasper Irvine
Ryde Academy, Ryde

Prison Break

I couldn't run for much longer, however, they were catching up. Sirens came from all around. What was I going to do? I was freaking out, it was dark by this point. As I edged through the forest, I knew it wasn't going to be long until I was caught. I sprinted into the forest. All I could see for miles were dead, gloomy trees. As I got further through the forest, I saw a pitch-black cave. I thought it would be a good hiding place. I was in the cave as footsteps neared...

Crystal-Rose Griffiths (13)
Ryde Academy, Ryde

Mafia Problems

I still have nightmares about it to this day. It was the time when I was being chased. It was the middle of the night when I heard knocking on the door. It was the mafia, they were hunting me down. I grabbed my gun and ran out the back door, blind terror making me run. I could run no more, so I hid behind a tree. I peeked just to hear them saying, "He must be here somewhere." I then took a shot and the bullet went through one's head. I then ran off into the distance...

Maciej Sadel (11)
Ryde Academy, Ryde

Drifting Down Under

It wasn't safe now they knew my secret. I thought I'd succeeded, but it was obvious I hadn't. The body, the river, I was there. I saw it all. They came to me in the dead of night, I told them I had no idea. Unfortunately, they didn't believe it. Shrieks of terror, screaming in pain, taking in water, she sank. I stared, unable to look away, and watched the now limp, lifeless body get submerged. We'd always hated each other, but now I felt they may hunt me and kill me...

Carla Harrison (13)
Ryde Academy, Ryde

Creature Or Human?

The sirens wailed as I ran. I could hear footsteps catching up to me. I knew I had to go somewhere where no one could find me. So many questions ran through my head. *Am I going to live or die? What's chasing me? Human or creature?* The footsteps disappeared. I was nearly there, nearly safe. Just a little more to go. At that moment, I heard a strong, deep, powerful howl from the forest. At last, I was safe. Then, I looked and it was face to face with me...

Ellie Carbin (14)
Ryde Academy, Ryde

Trapped

I had twenty-four hours to get out of this place. I felt like I was being watched and every move I'd made felt as if I'd done something wrong. I got to the open and saw something. I went to go and look at what it was. They were getting closer, so I rushed to the forest. They all split up. I was getting surrounded by them. I saw a break. I got some distance from them but, when I thought I was in the clear, they were all around me. I couldn't do anything. I saw it...

Jake Mander (13)
Ryde Academy, Ryde

Hunted

What was happening? I was running; I had been for what felt like years. All I had done was steal some bread and now six men were chasing me. I turned a corner and, without thinking, jumped into the local pub. It would be safer, even though it was eighteen and over only. The music in the pub stopped, everyone froze. "Get the scumbag!" I ran out of the pub as fast as my rapidly dying legs could go. Now, the angry mob from earlier was surrounding me... I was stuffed.

Jacob Orme (11)
Ryde Academy, Ryde

I'm Being Hunted!

I couldn't run for much longer. My palms were sweaty as blood dripped out of the cut on my leg. The sirens wailed as I sprinted down the soggy field, helicopters flashing their lights at me. There was a hole that made it stand out as a drain. "Surely no one will find me here, will they?" I asked myself.

As I went down there, it was nothing like I'd expected. It was a non-stop, deep tunnel. I hit the bottom. I was being hunted...

Jack Schubert (11)
Ryde Academy, Ryde

Hunted

We have to leave now, before it's too late. We need to get to the car. I don't know what is hunting us, a human or an animal, but whatever it is, we need to get to the car before it gets us. A loud bang goes off and then another. I look at my friend, he's not standing. He's lying on the floor, dead. I know I have to get out of there before I'm the same. I drop all my things and run like never before. Then, I see it, big and bold...

Jay Rayson
Ryde Academy, Ryde

The Mysterious Flick

The sirens wailed while twigs broke behind me. As I went further, it got louder and louder. I turned around and I was shocked to see a samurai sword covered with blood. Knowing that a man in a suit was behind me flicking a lighter constantly meant one thing: that I, the hunter, was being hunted. I turned around and I was stabbed, but no one was there. I fell to the ground, hoping not to be found but, before I knew it, it was too late to do anything...

Sammy Gallimore (11)
Ryde Academy, Ryde

Hunter

It's not safe now they know. I feel as if I can hear them, maybe it's other people, but I want to keep it safe. I need to move into the nearby forest. I can see them in my sight. I beg to God for them not to see me. They're coming this way. What will they do to me?

They walk past me. Now's my chance to go to the forest. They turn and spot me. *Go! Go!* I swear there's never a break from them. Then, I hear the police...

Pixie-Rose Sunshine Gardner (12)

Ryde Academy, Ryde

The Chase

The sirens wailed quite a distance away. We had to leave, now. I was now imagining what would happen if they found us. As I ran from the scene, I saw the gloom of a dark, dense forest, but then I caught a glimpse of light from the sun. I found a clearing of sand with a couple with a piece of tarpaulin over the top of them. I saw a hole next to them, the barking of the dogs convincing me to jump into it. Then, I woke up in bed. It was just a dream...

Toby Seddon
Ryde Academy, Ryde

On The Run!

I still have nightmares about it, the time I was on the run, I decamped and legged it out of there. As soon as I got out of the gates and into the world, the sirens wailed. I ducked down behind a boulder as they shot past, praying they didn't see me. At least I had the dark night sky on my side. I waited for a while for things to repose. It wasn't safe to go anywhere, now they knew what I'd done. I couldn't run any longer. I knew I was done for...

Aidan Partridge (13)
Ryde Academy, Ryde

Police Chase

I was inches away from getting into the dark forest. I could hear footsteps behind me, catching up. I kept on seeing blue flashing lights everywhere I turned. I felt like I couldn't run for much longer; they kept shouting at me. At this point, it was really dark. Therefore, I went to go and turn a corner, but I slipped. The police then caught me. I was terrified! Suddenly, I thought to myself, *how did I end up in this mess?*

Chloe Powell (13)
Ryde Academy, Ryde

Now Is The Time To Run

I couldn't run for much longer. They found my home and I had to run before they got me. I had twenty-four hours to get the money but I couldn't get it. I had to run. I was hiding in a bush, they were walking and looking for me. I waited for them to go, but they didn't. I was there for hours, then they went. I was safe for now, so I ran to the bus stop and I was about to get on the bus and they saw me. I was so scared...

Jacob Patterson (14)
Ryde Academy, Ryde

That Night...

I still have nightmares from that night, the night that showed his true colours. I still hear his voice ringing through my ears. "*Here's Johnny!*" I hear it so clearly like it's happening all over again. "Open up, let's play!" Then nothing. About a minute goes past and all I can see is an axe go through my door. That's when reality hits me, it's not a dream...

Tyria Lake (14)
Ryde Academy, Ryde

The Return Of The Vampires

The length of the field in front of me was crying with distress as the blood gushed through my veins. I felt the sour blood devour me. I had twenty-four hours to live. I couldn't run for much longer. My blood dripped down like sweat. I turned around and saw a blood-sucking vampire. They were coming... What should I do?

Katie Taylor (14)
Ryde Academy, Ryde

SOS

We were close, but still not close enough. I could feel the fury closing in, all the chaos consuming me. There was nowhere to run from this havoc, nowhere to hide from this madness. I felt like a hunted animal, followed closely, just waiting to be killed. The air scrambled out of me as I forced myself to run faster. The blood-shadow loomed so close behind, I could feel its breath burning my skin. An echo disappeared into the empty air, so calm yet so lethal. "Into the jaws of death. Into the mouth of hell. That's where you're going..."

Gurleen Kaur (13)
St Catherine's College, Eastbourne

Run

Heart pumping. Heart racing. Ears ringing. Mouth quivering. "Run!" his words echoed in my head. Where was he? Did he know? I missed him. I needed his help. I needed him. I wanted him. It was all a mess. My faith was scraping on the edge. *Run.* My legs were giving up and my heart was too. My likelihood of survival was dismally decreasing. My hopes shattered; I turned a corner to lose them. Did it work? Darkness tunnelled my vision. Darkness blackened my vision. I was falling... falling... I hoped I saved him... Were my efforts enough?

Lois Katie Hilton (15)
St Catherine's College, Eastbourne

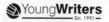

Twisting Terror

The sirens wailed and I jumped with fright. My dad yelled, "Get out! I'll get Wilson!" Adrenaline rushed through me like a lightning strike as I grabbed my most precious item. My mum's picture. Storming out the door, the whipping wind was gaining power by the second. We clawed our way along the ground, Dad dragging the shaking, whimpering dog. He was desperately trying to open the shelter door. Our lives depended on it. Bins, poles, rubbish flew by. I was yanked from the grip of the storm as the door clanged shut. We were safe... for the moment.

Josh Bolton (18)
Victoria Education Centre, Branksome Park

Hunted

I couldn't run for much longer. Each step I took felt like needles penetrating the dry, pale, wilting skin all over my feeble body. The sound of my bare feet hitting the cold stone floor echoed throughout the dark hallway, but it was just my footsteps that were echoing... the soul suckers' feet were echoing too. They were on the hunt for me, more importantly, my soul so they could just the remnants to fuel their sadistic experiments. Suddenly, I woke up, still tied down with needles stabbing me. It was a dream, there was no escape...

Elisha Robinson (17)
Victoria Education Centre, Branksome Park

Operation: The Hunt For The Zombie Werewolf Infection

He saw there was a SWAT truck chasing a Land Rover Defender, so he pulled out his Kel-Tech PMR 30 and fired at the SWAT truck. That officer shot the virus out of Jase's hand. It flew to the graveyard tomb belonging to Bob Howard, aka Bravo 8.

Bob came back to life and rushed out of the graveyard. Security agents raced to the entrance with 9mms. The werewolf-zombies were pushing hard to get inside. Luckily, they blew up the werewolf-zombies with RPGs and America was saved. Jase Detroit was sentenced to twenty years in jail.

Christopher Jones (17)
Victoria Education Centre, Branksome Park

The Game Glitch

The game started glitching. I was almost sick. Next, I could feel the cold floor. I could smell oil. I could see their eyes in the dark. I could hear their footsteps. I knew I couldn't run. I turned to the left, switching on the light, and there was one of the giant robotic beasts standing right there in the doorway. I slammed the huge metal door just in time for another one to come running towards the door. I wasn't so lucky this time. Picking me up from the ground, it opened its mouth wide... Game over.

Louis Meddelton (16)
Victoria Education Centre, Branksome Park

Hunted!

I couldn't run for much longer. I knew if I stopped, they would be on me quicker than kids running for the last chocolate bar in the shop. They knew that I had what they wanted, but I wasn't going to give it up that easily. I kept running but something inside me told me it was going to end and not in a good way. I hid behind the big bin outside the back door of a restaurant. The air was getting colder like it always did when the hunt was on. I made myself as small as possible...

Charlotte Sharpe (17)
Victoria Education Centre, Branksome Park

Five Hundred Zombies

Five hundred zombies chasing him. He had run for five hours. He was really tired and stressed. His mum beeped the horn of her monster truck and he got in. They mowed down the zombies and killed them. As they got away, they hit a post and crashed...

Deniz Akgul (13)
Victoria Education Centre, Branksome Park

Chaos

Midnight. Chaos. If my childhood-self saw this, she'd never consider living in London. Standing up from my knees, I crept towards the bushes, peeping through the cracks. The coast was clear. My big moment commenced. I sped onto the path running madly. I felt so free although I didn't process what was happening. I heard a bark. Glancing behind... a policeman, a German shepherd wearing a uniform was chasing me! Ignoring him, I ran faster. My legs, uncontrollable; my mind, frantic. I stopped.
Unexpectedly, a huge weight grabbed my shoulder. Towards my left, a colossal, hairy hand... The policeman.

Imaniya Hussain (11)
Woking High School, Horsell

Hunted

Breathing heavily, I ran in the dull and isolated tunnel. As I was running to the tunnel, my heart was pounding fast. I stood still. Bending down and clenching my knees, trying to get my breath, I heard a noise. I turned around, seeing if anyone was there. It was empty. I looked down again, trying to catch my breath. I heard the noise again. Thinking to myself, *where are they coming from?* I hesitantly looked up. My heart stopped. I froze. Two red balloons. "Argh!" It felt like someone was behind me, strangling me...

Sana Newa Khan (11)
Woking High School, Horsell

Hunted

Blood filled my mouth. Branches tore at my dress and roots dared to trip me up. My heart didn't seem to beat as I ran through the woods, glancing over my shoulder, the damp air filling my lungs. A rock sliced through my finger and blood spurted from the gash. I could hear them behind me and I quickly hid behind a boulder as the car sped past. However, I could never escape from who I was and where I'd come from...

Chloe Isabella Barwick (11)
Woking High School, Horsell

YOUNG WRITERS INFORMATION

We hope you have enjoyed reading this book – and that you will continue to in the coming years.

If you're a young writer who enjoys reading and creative writing, or the parent of an enthusiastic poet or story writer, do visit our website **www.youngwriters.co.uk**. Here you will find free competitions, workshops and games, as well as recommended reads, a poetry glossary and our blog. There's lots to keep budding writers motivated to write!

If you would like to order further copies of this book, or any of our other titles, then please give us a call or order via your online account.

Young Writers
Remus House
Coltsfoot Drive
Peterborough
PE2 9BF
(01733) 890066
info@youngwriters.co.uk

Join in the conversation!
Tips, news, giveaways and much more!

YoungWritersUK   @YoungWritersCW